In memory of Ernest

Oxford University Press, Walton Street, Oxford OX2 6DP

Oxford New York
Athens Auckland Bangkok Bombay
Calcutta Cape Town Dar es Salaam Delhi
Florence Hong Kong Istanbul Karachi
Kuala Lumpur Madras Madrid Melbourne
Mexico City Nairobi Paris Singapore
Taipei Tokyo Toronto

and associated companies in
Berlin Ibadan

Oxford is a trade mark of Oxford University Press

Copyright © Sheila Isherwood 1994
Illustrations © Kate Isherwood 1994
First published 1994
First published in paperback 1996

A CIP catalogue record for this book is available
from the British Library

ISBN 0 19 279974 6 (hardback)
ISBN 0 19 272150 X (paperback)

Typeset in Monotype Bembo by Pentacor PLC., High Wycombe, Bucks
Printed in Hong Kong

My Grandad

SHEILA ISHERWOOD

Illustrated by
KATE ISHERWOOD

Oxford University Press

When I was four years old, my grandad gave me a very special birthday present; my pet rabbit called Gretchen. She's the best present I've ever had. I love to lie on the grass in our garden and talk to her, even though I know she doesn't understand what I say. And when she twitches her nose and looks up at me, I always think of Grandad.

You see, my grandad was much older than other grandads. He was so old that one day it was his time to die. But I love to remember the time when he lived, because then we did all sorts of interesting things together, especially in the garden. That was Grandad's favourite place. When I was very little, I used to go out with him, even on cold and windy days, to pull up a cabbage, or to dig, or to tidy up the mess the wind always made.

The spring and summer were Grandad's busiest times. He spent every day in his garden sowing seeds and planting out vegetables. He weeded and watered them so that they grew big, and fat enough for us to eat. Mummy used to laugh and joke and say the garden was so crowded with growing plants it was like a jungle, and she had quite a job finding us among them.

Then, sometimes, Grandad and I would surprise her. We would pick all the ripe pea-pods we could find and shell them ready for dinner. We used to count the peas one by one as they popped and bounced into the basin—and out of it! Sometimes I used to eat the raw peas, crunching them in my mouth, and Grandad used to smile and wink and pretend he hadn't seen me.

But of all the things Grandad grew in his garden, the strawberries were the best—the most delicious. Huge, red, juicy strawberries that we used to eat for tea with spoonfuls of clotted cream on top. Hundreds of them! If ever there were too many for tea, we ate the rest for breakfast the next morning.

I remember other things about Grandad, too, like the times we used to go shopping together, or when, holding on to his hand, I used to go with him into his bank. I liked the bank. It was at the top of some long, high steps that were hard to climb; and it had a ceiling that went right up into the sky. It felt very important.

And then I remember Sundays when Grandad spent the whole day with us, especially the Sunday when he brought me my 'surprise' birthday present. I had to close my eyes tightly. 'No peeping,' Grandad said, as he carried me into the garden. He put me down, then said, 'Now you can look!' I unscrewed my eyes and there in front of me was a baby rabbit nibbling busily on some chopped carrots and lettuce leaves.

'She's for you,' Grandad said. I couldn't believe it. I hugged and kissed Grandad and promised him that I would always love her and take care of her.

Best of all, Grandad used to make me laugh. Once, when Daddy was working, Grandad, Mummy, and I had a picnic beside a field—a field full of cows munching on the long grass. We were on our way to look at a house that was for sale, many miles away in the middle of the countryside. While we sat on a rug and ate cheese and tomato sandwiches for lunch, I remember watching Grandad put his hat on the top of his car. 'It will be safe up there,' he said.

Well, when we finished our picnic, Grandad took me across to a wooden gate and lifted me on to it so that I could see, more easily, the cows grazing in the field. They saw me and came right up close to the gate with their black eyes staring at me and their pink noses so near I could have stretched my hand out and touched them! But I didn't.

As soon as the picnic things were packed into the back of the car again, we drove away. When, at last, we came to the house for sale, I suddenly noticed that Grandad didn't have his hat on his head. We had forgotten it was on the roof of the car, even Mummy. Then we realized that it must have blown away on the wind when the car moved. Grandad was sad at first, but soon he began to laugh so much he made me laugh as well.

He laughed and he laughed. He was still laughing when he said, 'A cow might have it on its head, or a sheep.' He laughed some more and said, 'Or a pig, or even a goat.' The thought of a cow wearing Grandad's hat was very funny, so funny that I, too, couldn't stop laughing for a long time.

Even now when I remember it, I begin to laugh.

So, you see, I still have my grandad in many ways, even though he died.